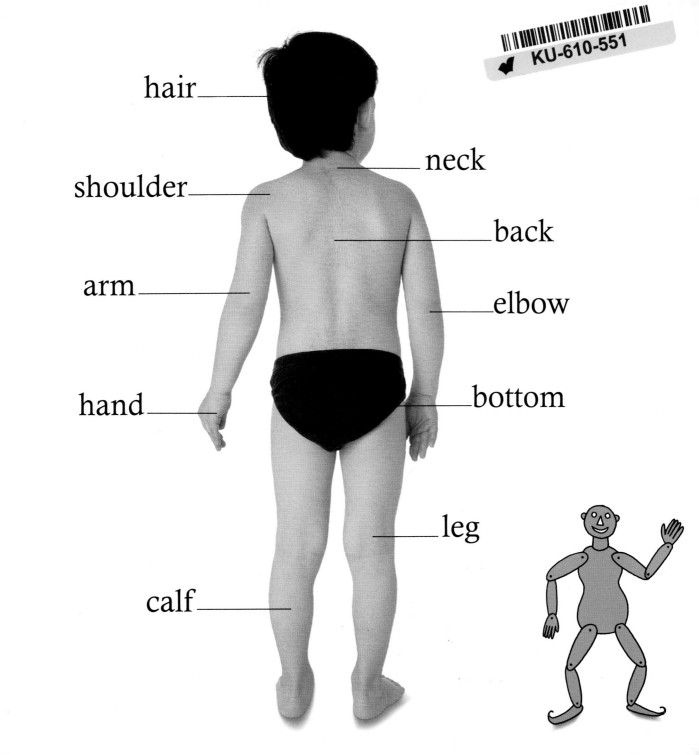

hair

neck

shoulder

back

arm

elbow

hand

bottom

leg

calf

Skin and bones

Your body is covered in smooth skin. Inside your body are your bones. Your bones are joined together to make your skeleton.

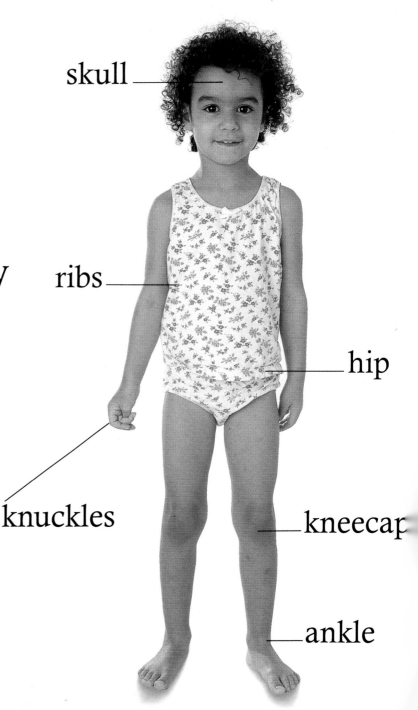

skull

ribs

hip

knuckles

kneecap

ankle

Funny bones

See if you can feel these bones. Press hard!

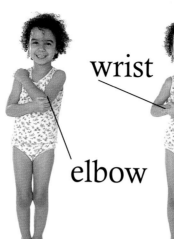

wrist

elbow

knee

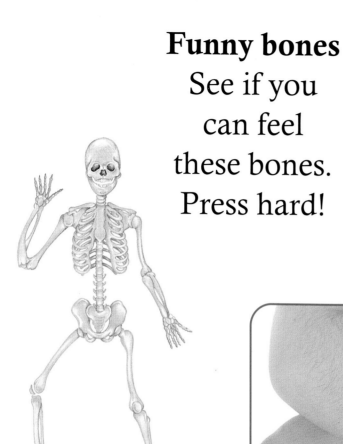

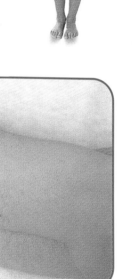

Your skeleton

Without your skeleton, you would be a big blob!

Skin

Most of your skin has short, soft hair on it. Can you feel the hairs on your skin?

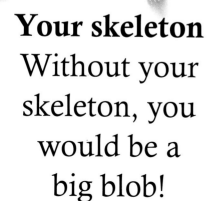

Mouth

Your mouth is for talking, eating and smiling!

Talking

You move your tongue and your lips to talk.

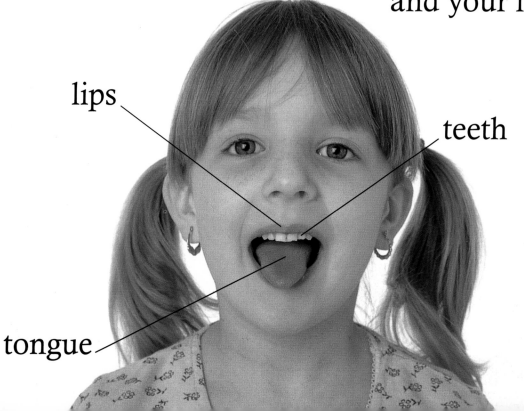

lips

teeth

tongue

Eating

You use your teeth to take a bite of food.

You use your tongue to taste your food.

After chewing your food, you swallow it.

Smiling

A smile says, "Hello, it's nice to see you". Who smiles at you?

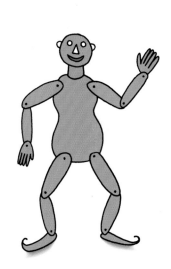

Eyes

You use your eyes to see all around you. When you are sad or hurt, tears fall from your eyes.

eyelashes

eyebrow

eyelid

eye

pupil

Eye colours
Eyes can be different colours. What colour are your eyes?

grey eyes

Wearing glasses

Glasses help eyes to work better. Do you wear glasses?

Crying

When you cry your eyes make salty tears. Do you cry sometimes?

blue eyes

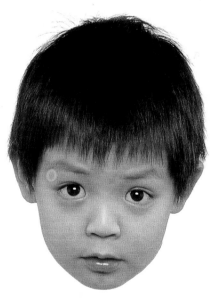

brown eyes

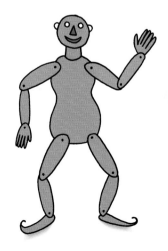

Nose

You use your nose to smell things. You sneeze with your nose, too.

Do these things smell nice or nasty?

perfume

onion

herbs

pasta

nose

nostril

cat food

What do you like to smell?

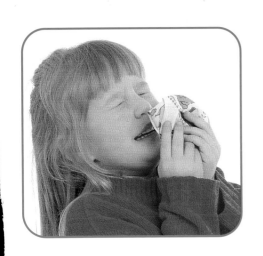

Atishoo!

Sometimes, sneezing means
that you have a cold.
What makes you sneeze?

cat

shark

dog

Animal noses

All these animals
use their noses to help
them find food.

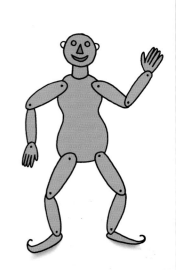

Ears

You use your ears to hear all the noises around you.

Different noises

What noises do these things make?

drum

baby crying

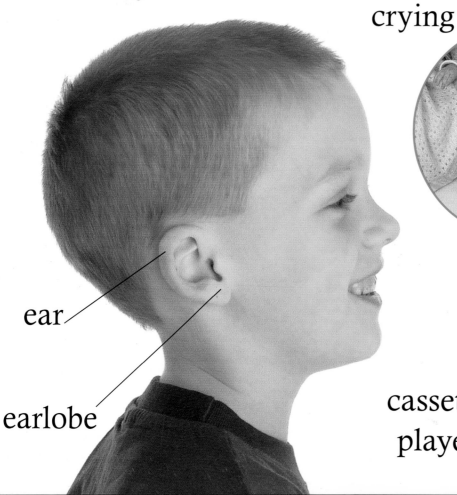

ear

earlobe

cassette player

clapping

handbells

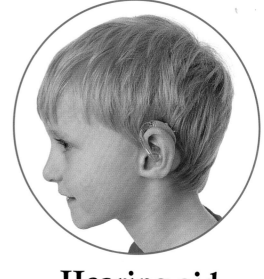

Hearing aid
Some people use a hearing aid to help their ears work better.

Listening
You use your ears to listen to stories.

Can you hear any noises?

Hands

You use your hands to hold, touch and feel things.

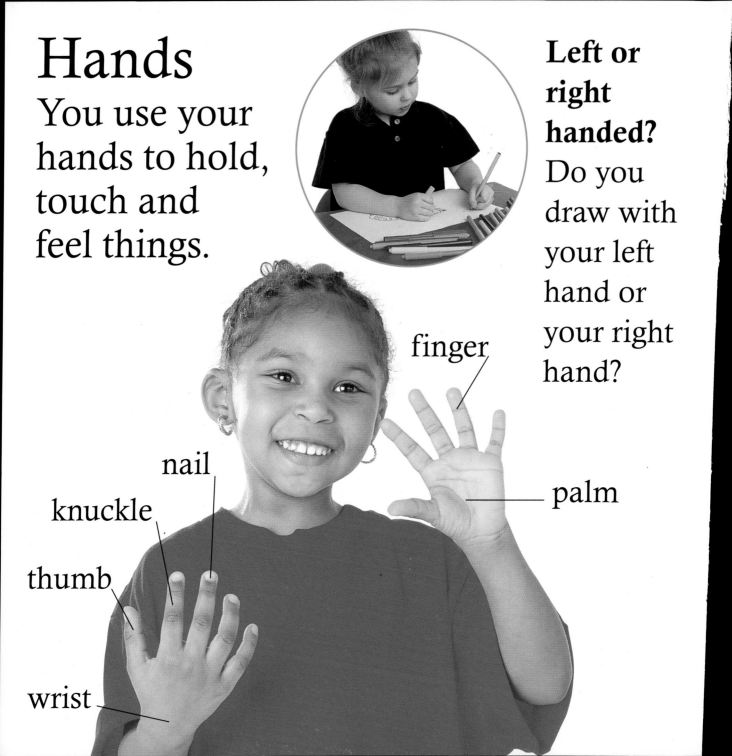

Left or right handed? Do you draw with your left hand or your right hand?

finger

nail

knuckle

thumb

palm

wrist

Helping hands

Look at all these things your hands help you to do. Can you think of some more?

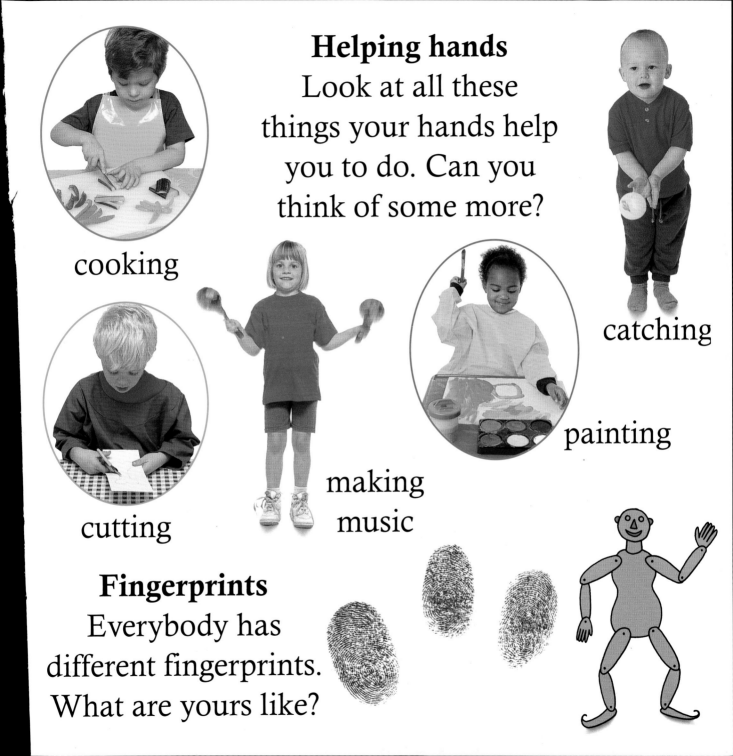

cooking

catching

cutting

making music

painting

Fingerprints

Everybody has different fingerprints. What are yours like?

Arms and legs

Your arms and legs
help you to walk,
run, jump, dance
and play games.

dancing

skipping

throwing

Which of these things can you do?

kicking

hopping

riding

Animal bodies

Animals have different bodies to help them do different things.

Long tail

A monkey's long tail helps it to balance on tree branches.

monkey

Slippery scales

Smooth, slippery scales help a snake to slither along the ground.

snake

frog

Feathery wings
A bird could not fly without its strong, light wings.

Strong legs
A frog's strong back legs help it to jump high into the air.

seagull

sea-lion

Smooth shape
A sea-lion's smooth body and strong tail help it to swim.

Make them match

Can you match the right words to the pictures?

smiling

throwing

eating

hopping

cooking